Balloons Fly By

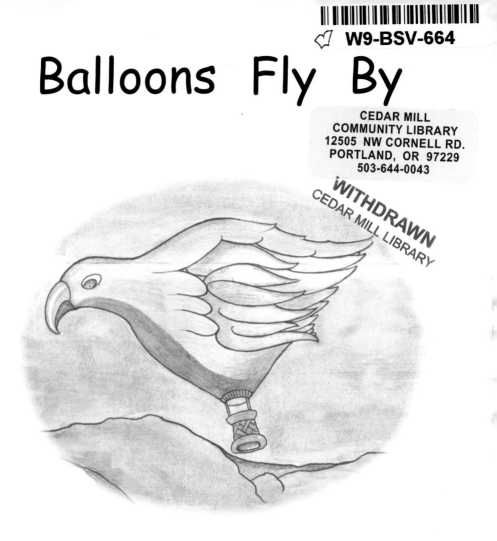

written by Pam Holden
illustrated by Tiare Dickson

1

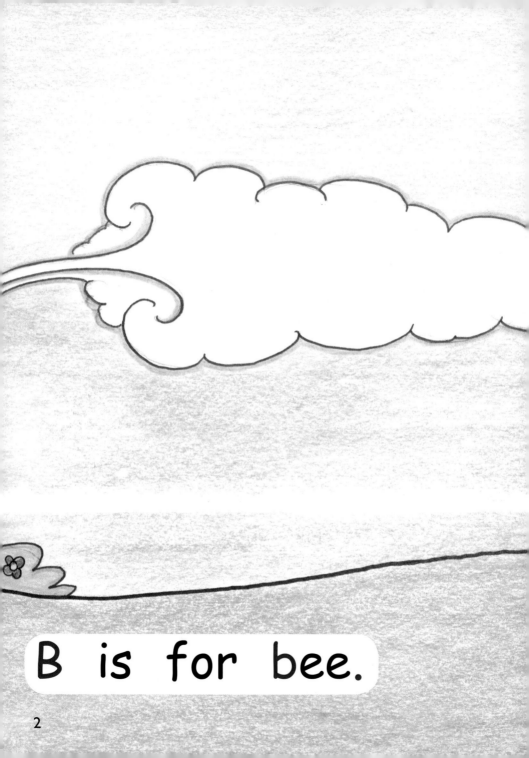

B is for bee.

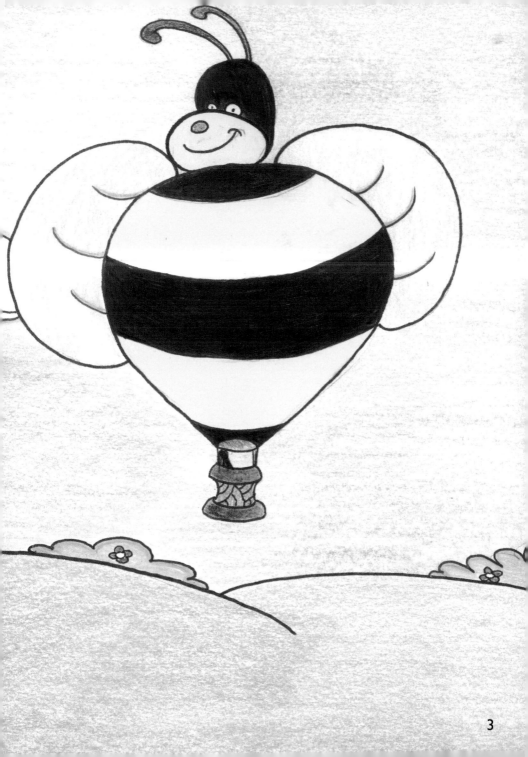

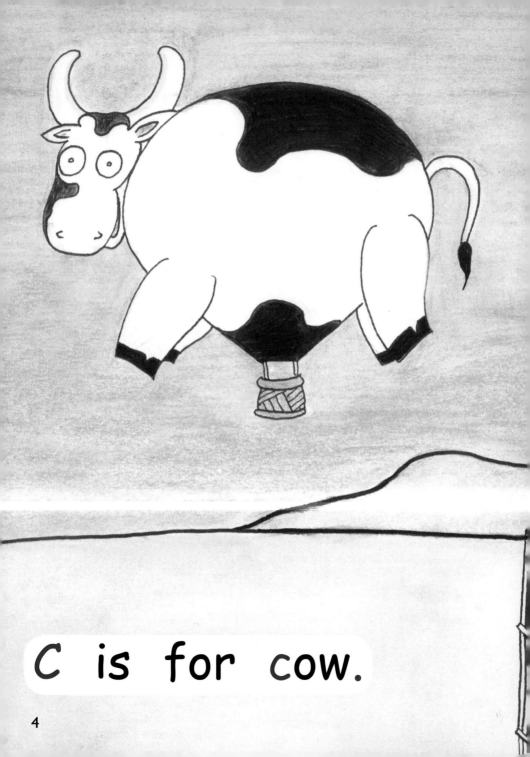

C is for cow.

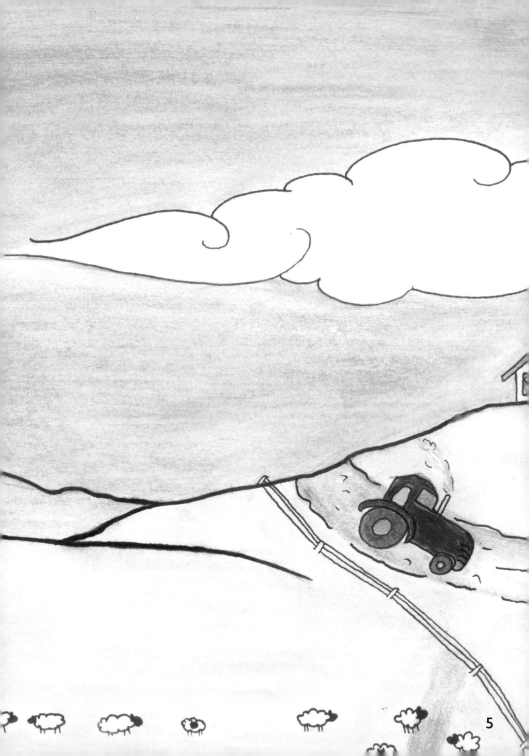

L is for ladybug.

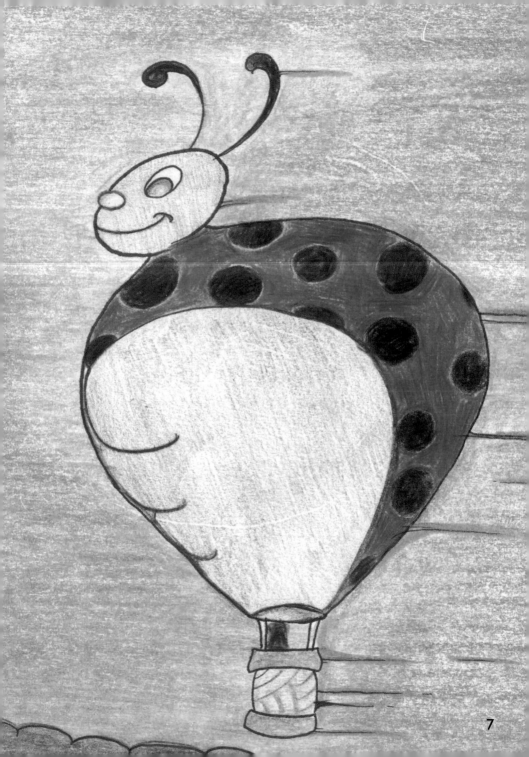

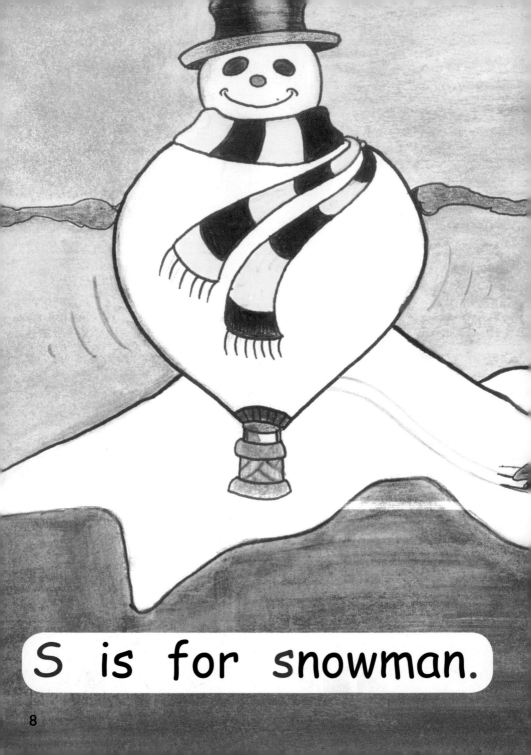

S is for snowman.

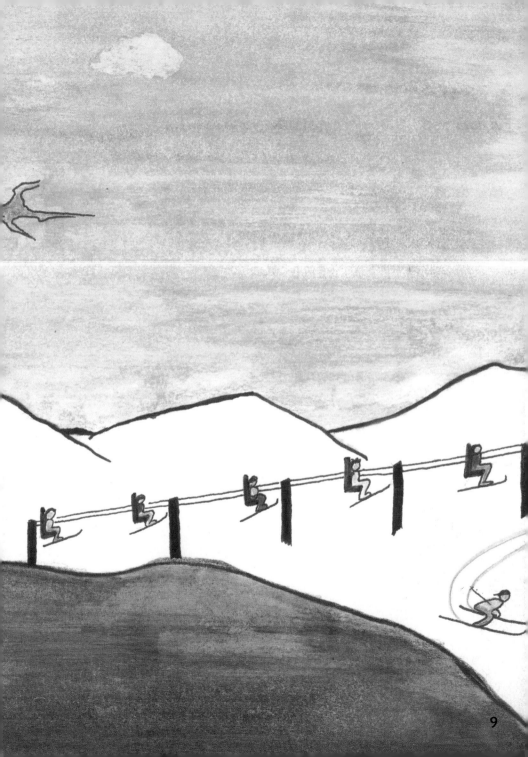

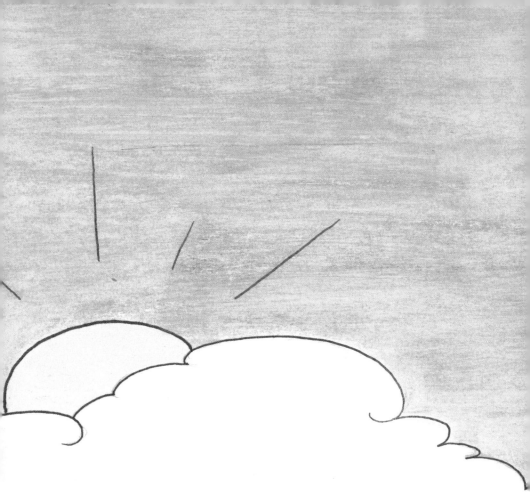

B is for
birthday cake.

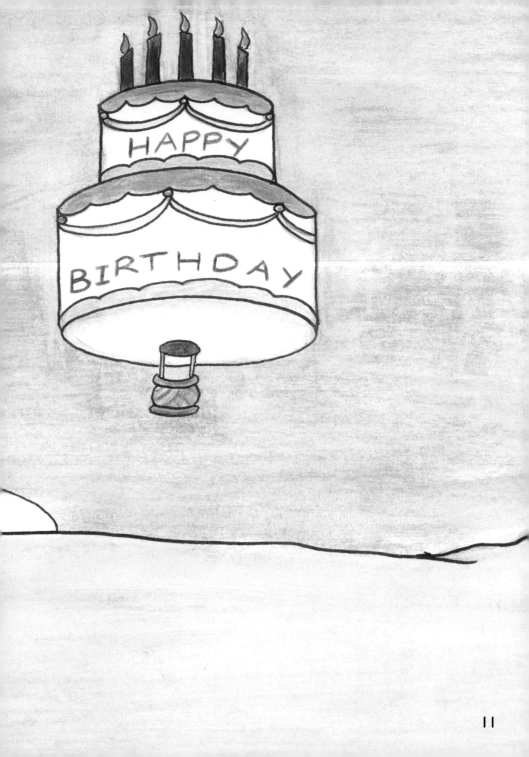

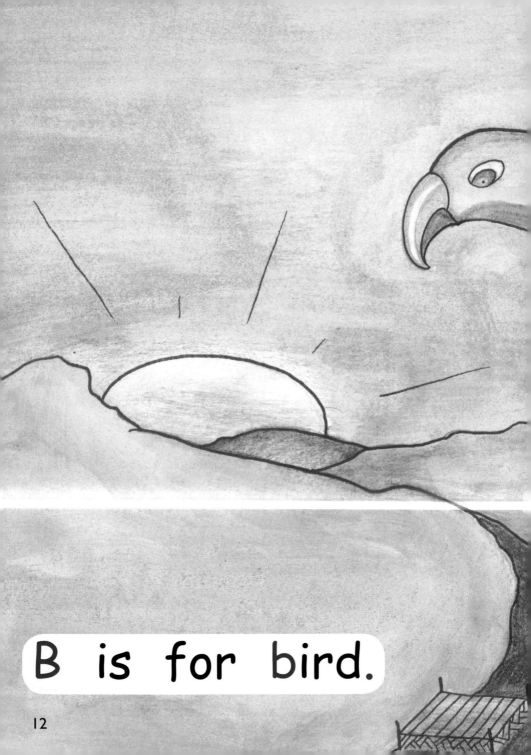

B is for bird.

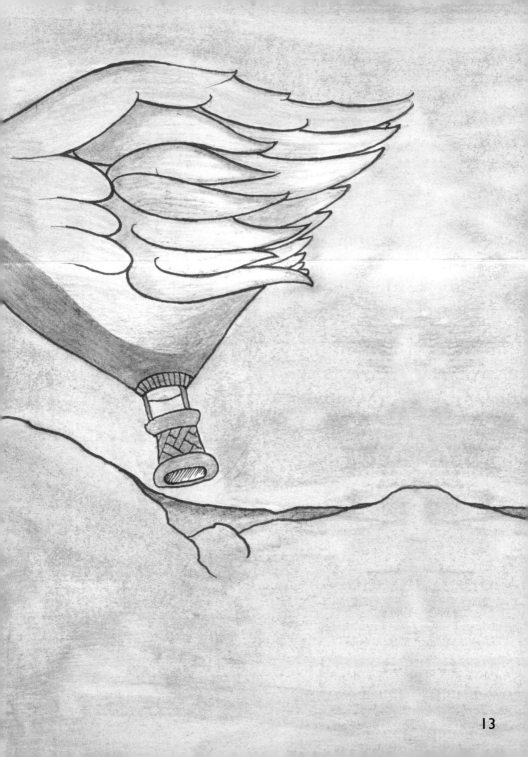

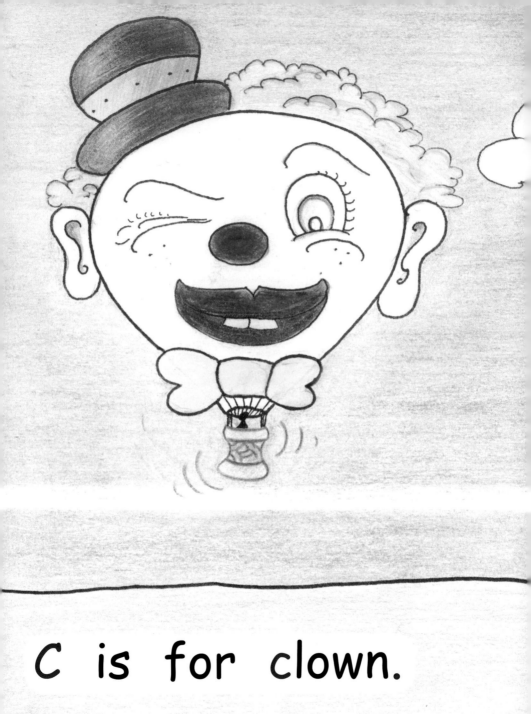

C is for clown.

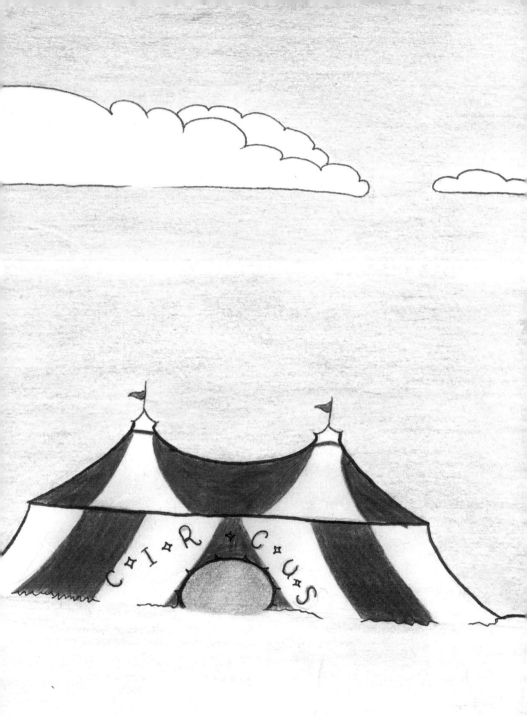

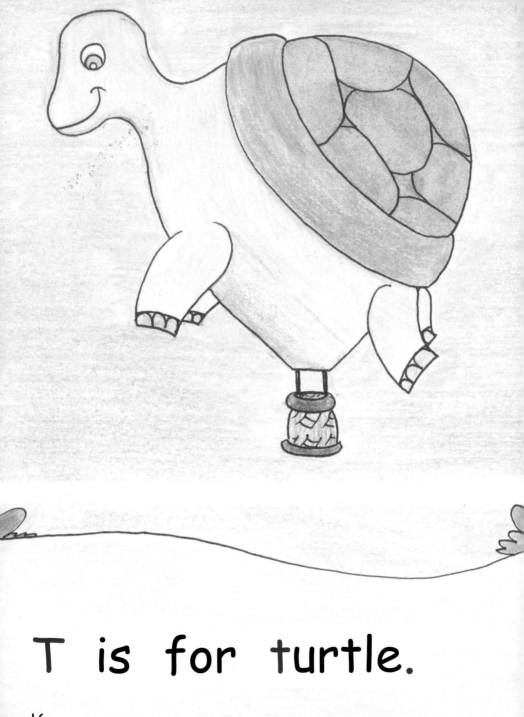

T is for turtle.